Leo
All Alone

Also by Holly Webb:
Max the Missing Puppy
Ginger the Stray Kitten
Buttons the Runaway Puppy
The Frightened Kitten
Jessie the Lonely Puppy
The Kitten Nobody Wanted
Harry the Homeless Puppy
Lost in the Snow
The Brave Kitten
Sky the Unwanted Kitten
The Secret Puppy
Little Puppy Lost

Leo
All Alone

by Holly Webb
Illustrated by Sophy Williams

tiger tales

For Alice, Max, and Georgie

tiger tales

5 River Road, Suite 128, Wilton, CT 06897
Published in the United States 2016
Originally published in Great Britain 2007
by Little Tiger Press
Text copyright © 2007 Holly Webb
Illustrations copyright © 2007 Sophy Williams
ISBN-13: 978-1-68010-016-7
ISBN-10: 1-68010-016-5
Printed in China
STP/1800/0075/0815
All rights reserved
10 9 8 7 6 5 4 3 2 1

For more insight and activities, visit us at www.tigertalesbooks.com

Chapter One

"Evie, did you put these in the shopping cart?" Evie's mom was staring at a packet of rice cakes, looking confused.

"No. Why would I, Mom? They look horrible." Evie made a face. "It was you, don't you remember? You said they might be nice to nibble on when you were feeling sick. But I bet they'll just make you feel even more sick."

Her mom sighed. "You're probably right." She smiled apologetically at the cashier, who was waiting for them to pay. "Sorry. I seem to be a bit forgetful at the moment."

The girl smiled back. "That's okay. My sister's pregnant and she locked herself out of the house twice last week. How long until the baby's due?"

"Another nine weeks." Evie's mom sighed again. "The time just seems to be creeping by at the moment." She patted her enormous tummy.

"Mom, can I go and look at the bulletin board?" Evie asked. She was getting bored with baby talk. Ever since her mom's bump had begun to show, complete strangers had started talking to them in the street, asking about the baby. They always asked Evie how she felt about having a little brother or sister, and she was sick of having to smile and say she was looking forward to it. She was, but the attention was starting to get on her nerves. And she had a horrible feeling that it would get a lot worse after the baby arrived.

"Of course you can. Actually, Evie, see if anyone's selling any baby stuff. It would be a good way to find some bargains."

Evie sighed quietly. Honestly, did Mom ever think about anything else? She wandered over to the big board behind the Customer Service desk where they put up the advertisements. You could find some really fun things sometimes.

Once she'd spotted an advertisement for a pair of almost-new roller blades that someone had grown out of. She'd been able to afford them with her own money, and they were great.

She browsed through vacuum cleaners, lawn mowers, a girl offering to babysit — and then caught her breath in delight. The next ad was larger than some of the others, and it had a photo attached — a basket of the cutest little white puppies, all climbing over each other. One of them was grinning out at Evie, a naughty glint in his eye.

8

WESTIE PUPPIES READY FOR HOMES **NOW** REASONABLE PRICE

Call Mrs. Wilson at 555-2961

Evie sighed adoringly. That puppy was beautiful! She had to show him to Mom. She looked back over at the line to see if she was done yet. Her mom was looking around for her, and Evie waved, and then dashed over.

"Come and see! You'll love it. Anyway, you shouldn't be pushing that on your own, Mom. Dad would be really angry." Evie helped her mom with the cart, giving her a stern glare.

"Dad worries too much," Mom chuckled. "What am I looking at?" She stared at the board, trying to figure out what Evie was so excited about. "We're not buying a trampoline, Evie," she said, grinning. "And we definitely don't want a speedboat!"

"No, look, I just wanted you to see this cute photo." Evie pointed out the basket of puppies. "Aren't they sweet?"

"Oh, yes, they're beautiful. What kind of dog are they? Westies...." Mom gazed thoughtfully at the photo. "Westies are small dogs, aren't they?" she mused quietly.

Evie nodded. "I think Mrs. Jackson down the road has a Westie. You know, Tyson? He's so cute."

"Mmmm." Evie's mom nodded. "Okay. I suppose you're going to insist on pushing this shopping cart now, aren't you? Actually, Evie, do you want to go and look at the animal magazines? I have to go to the restroom again." She sighed theatrically. "Stay by the magazines. I'll only be a minute."

As soon as Evie set off, her mom searched hastily in her purse for a pen. Then she made a note of the name and phone number from the puppy advertisement on her receipt, and hurried after Evie.

As they drove home, Evie gazed out of the window, daydreaming about puppies. She had no idea that her mom was sneaking glances at her every so often. Over the last few weeks, Evie's mom and dad had been worrying about how the new baby was going to affect her. After all, eight was quite old to suddenly have a new baby brother or sister. Evie seemed to be happy about it, but it was difficult to tell. They'd been wondering what they could do to keep her from feeling left out, and it was only the day before that Evie's dad had thought of getting her a puppy. Her mom hadn't been too sure.

"Won't it be a lot of hassle, just before the baby comes?" she'd worried.

"We've got a few weeks. And the point is that Evie would be taking care of the puppy. It'll give her something to fuss over when we're fussing over the baby." Evie's dad was really enthusiastic. He liked dogs, and he knew Evie would love a puppy. After all, a puppy had been at the top of her Christmas list for the last three years. Her parents had always said she wasn't quite old enough — mostly because Evie's mom thought having a dog would be a lot of work. But Evie's dad had been trying hard to convince her, so the Westie ad had turned up at the perfect time.

"What are you thinking about, Evie?" Mom asked her, smiling. "You're miles away."

Evie grinned. "Just that adorable puppy. I know we can't have one, but if we did, I'd like one just like him...."

Evie's dad got home just in time to help make dinner, and Evie told him about the little white dog as she was setting the table.

"Puppies? For sale now?" he asked thoughtfully.

Evie saw him exchange a glance with her mom and caught her breath, her eyes widening in sudden hope. She looked back and forth between them. Her dad was grinning. "Funny that you saw that ad today, Evie. Your mom and I were talking last night. We've been thinking about getting you a dog, and now seems to be the right time."

Evie could hardly believe her ears.

"You mean it?" she breathed delightedly.

Mom nodded. "If you think you can take care of a dog properly. It's a big responsibility."

Evie nodded so hard that she made her neck ache. "I know, I know. I can!"

Mom smiled. "So, shall I call the lady with those puppies? You'd like a Westie?"

Evie just gaped at them. She'd wanted a dog for so long, and her parents had always said, "Maybe," and "Perhaps when you're older." Then she suddenly realized what her mom had just said and squeaked, "Yes! Yes, please!"

Evie hardly ate any dinner. She watched her parents, eating impatiently, and when her dad had swallowed his last mouthful of pasta, she snatched the plate away to put in the dishwasher.

"Hey! Evie! I was going to have seconds!" He smiled. "Okay, okay. Let's put you out of your misery."

Evie waited anxiously while her mom called the number. What if all the puppies were gone? After all, they didn't know how long the advertisement had been up there. She sat on the stair listening to her mom. It was hard to tell what was going on, but eventually her mom said, "Great. Well, we'll come around tomorrow morning. Thanks!" and then she put the phone down and beamed at Evie.

"I'm getting a puppy!" Evie gasped, jumping up and down in excitement. "I can't believe it! I have to go over and tell Grandma!"

Evie's grandma lived a couple of

streets away with her own two dogs, Ben the Spaniel, and Tigger, who was a Greyhound cross with crazy stripes. Evie heard them barking madly as she rang the doorbell. She grinned to herself. She couldn't wait to introduce Ben and Tigger to her new puppy!

"Guess what, guess what!" she announced as Grandma opened the door. "I'm getting a dog!" She didn't manage to say much after that as Tigger was jumping up and trying to lick her face.

"Down, Tigger! Stop it, silly boy. It's only Evie; you see her every day!" Grandma shooed the dogs away and went into the kitchen to put the kettle on. "Darling, did you say you were getting a dog?"

"A puppy! Mom and Dad are giving me a puppy — we're going to pick one out tomorrow morning." Evie sighed blissfully. She wasn't sure she could wait that long.

Grandma looked confused. "But … just before the baby arrives?"

Evie nodded happily. Then she leaned over the table, lowering her voice as though she were telling secrets. "They didn't say, but I think it's to make me feel better about the baby," she explained.

Her grandma nodded thoughtfully. "Well, everyone would understand if you found it difficult, Evie, you know that, don't you?"

"Grandma, you know I'm really looking forward to it." Evie laughed.

"And now I'll have a puppy, too!" She beamed at Grandma, expecting her to be really excited. But Grandma was stirring her tea thoughtfully. "What's the matter?" Evie asked, frowning.

"Nothing, Evie. It's wonderful news. It's just…." Grandma sipped her tea, thinking about what to say. "I'm just wondering if this is the right time. With the baby coming. A new puppy will be a lot of work, you know."

Evie shook her head. "Don't worry. I know about taking care of dogs from helping with Ben and Tigger, and Dad knows a lot about them, too." Evie bent down to scratch Tigger behind his ears, so she didn't see her grandma's worried face. "I've wanted a dog for so long! I still can't believe it's really happening!" Evie gave Tigger an excited hug. Tomorrow she was going to meet her own puppy for the first time!

Chapter Two

Evie just couldn't stay in bed the next morning. She usually loved sleeping in on Saturdays after getting up for school all week, but today she was much too excited. She hardly ate any breakfast, either — she just stirred her chocolate cereal in circles until it looked like mud.

"You might as well eat it, you know,

Evie," her mom pointed out, slowly buttering a piece of toast. "We're not going yet. I told Mrs. Wilson we'd be there at 10."

"But that's hours away!" Evie wailed.

"Mrs. Wilson has to feed the puppies and get everything ready," her mom explained. "We can't go over there before then."

"I suppose," Evie agreed reluctantly. She trailed upstairs, wondering what she was going to do to fill an entire hour before they could leave. Then she had an idea. She'd go and look up puppies on the internet to try and find out about taking care of a dog. Evie settled down at the computer and before long was busy making notes. By the time her mom called her downstairs, Evie's head was bursting with information about feeding, walking, vaccinations, and training. It was a lot to think about. But she knew she could do it!

"Oh, look! He's all shy!" Evie giggled, and stretched out her hand to the fluffy white puppy who was peeking out at her around his mother. He took a step back, then curiosity got the better of him. Tail slowly wagging, he began to sneak forward to where Evie was sitting on the floor.

"He's a little cutie, that one, probably my favorite," Mrs. Wilson said fondly. "I'm going to miss him — he's such a sweet-natured dog."

Mom shook her head. "I don't know
how you can bear to see them go.
They're all so beautiful." She scratched
the puppy she was cuddling under the
chin, and the little dog snuffled happily
at her fingers.

"Well, this is the last time I'll have to, actually." Mrs. Wilson sighed. "Lady and I are getting too old for puppies! We're retiring, aren't we, my special girl?" She patted the puppies' mother, a beautiful snow-white dog with melting brown eyes. "We're going to live by the sea. Lady loves walking along the beach. And getting soaking wet!"

Evie could have sworn that Lady's eyes sparkled naughtily. That was the amazing thing about her and the puppies — they all seemed so bright and intelligent. Then the fluffy little boy puppy suddenly nuzzled at her hand, and she squeaked in delight. She'd been watching Lady and hadn't noticed him creeping up on her.

"He seems to have taken a liking to

you, Evie." Dad laughed, watching the puppy chasing Evie's fingers as she danced her hand up and down.

Evie nodded, and then looked seriously at both Mom and Dad. "Is it really up to me to choose?" she asked worriedly. "I mean, all four of them are wonderful."

"It's a hard job," Dad agreed. "But we can't take them all."

Evie giggled as the little boy puppy scrambled up her jeans, trying to climb into her lap. She helped him out with a boost under his little back paws, and he heaved himself up. Then he turned around four times, gave a great sigh of satisfaction, and went to sleep curled up tight in a little white ball.

Evie looked up, her eyes glowing. "This one," she said firmly.

"Mmm, I don't think you had much choice," Dad agreed, smiling. "He's definitely chosen you! Now you just have to think of a name for him."

Evie smiled. "I know what I'm going to call him. His name is Leo."

Mom and Dad gazed at the little puppy. "That's a perfect name," said Mom. "He looks just like a Leo."

It was so difficult to leave Leo behind, but Evie knew she'd see him again the next day. He'd be coming home with them! Now they just had to get everything they needed to take care of him. Mrs. Wilson had given them a list, and Evie studied it in the car on the way to the pet store.

"Basket. Food bowl. Water bowl. Collar. Leash. Harness. Chew toys," she muttered.

Dad sighed. "Nearly as bad as the baby," he moaned. "You sure little Leo doesn't need a bassinet as well, Evie?"

It was so exciting later that afternoon to see the basket with its bright red cushion waiting in a warm spot in the kitchen, and the collar and leash hanging from one of the hooks in the hallway. Everything was ready for Leo to come home.

"Oh, look! He's found his new basket!"

Evie and her parents were watching Leo explore his new home. He was trotting around on unsteady paws, sniffing at everything.

"Ah-choo!" Leo sneezed and stepped back, shaking his head.

"Oops!" said Dad. "I didn't know my boots smelled that bad. Let's leave him to settle in."

That night, Evie sneaked back down to the kitchen after her bedtime to check that Leo was okay. He'd eaten all his dinner and seemed to have made himself at home, but she was worried that he would be lonely, since he was used to sleeping with his mom and his brother and sisters. Leo had been lying awake. He'd been trying to make sense of all the strange things that had been happening that day. His first car ride; the new house; a new basket to sleep in.

And new people. They seemed very nice — the girl smelled friendly, which was important.

The door clicked open softly, and Leo's ears pricked up. It was the girl, Evie. "Shhh!" she whispered. "We can't let Mom and Dad hear us, Leo. You're supposed to stay in your basket, but I bet you're scared down here on your own. I'm taking you up to my bedroom instead. Mrs. Wilson said you were very well house-trained, so I'll put some newspaper down for you, okay? Mom would be upset if you peed on my rug!" She snuggled him close as they crept up the stairs, and Leo settled into her arms. This was much better than a basket, even a nice one like he'd been given.

Of course, Evie's mom and dad soon figured out exactly what was going on, but they were so glad that Leo was settling in, and making Evie so happy, that they pretended not to notice. From that night on, Leo slept on Evie's bed every night, snoring gently.

It didn't take long for Leo to become part of the family. He was such a friendly little dog. After a couple of weeks, when he'd had all his shots, he was allowed to go out for walks, which meant he could go to school to pick up Evie. She loved coming out to see Mom waiting with Leo on his bright red leash. Usually it was twisted all around his paws and he tripped over it as he tried to race over to her. Her friends were all really jealous, and Leo got petted by everyone. Then they'd head home and Leo would watch TV with Evie on the sofa. He soon decided on his favorite programs, and he got very good at singing along to the theme songs in a howl.

Mom hadn't been so sure about getting a dog, but Leo won her over very quickly. He loved people, and he followed her around the house as she did the housework. He was much better company than the radio! And whenever she sat down, he rested his head on her feet.

Of course, Leo didn't have to work hard to charm Evie's grandma. She was always popping over to see him and Evie, and it was great to have her to ask about dog-training tips. It only took

Leo a few days to learn about asking to go outside and Grandma warned Evie not to give him too many doggy treats as a reward, as he was starting to look a little chubby!

Once Leo could meet up with other dogs, Evie took him over to Grandma's house to be introduced to Ben and Tigger. Leo was a little shy at first — they were a lot bigger than he was, especially Tigger — but after half an hour he was chasing them around the yard. Ben the Spaniel soon figured out a good way to calm Leo down when he was being too excitable — he sat on him! Evie panicked the first time he did it, but Grandma said it would probably be good for Leo to have an older dog bossing him around, and that Ben wouldn't hurt him.

Evie and Dad soon got into the habit of taking Leo for an evening walk after dinner. It gave Mom the chance to snooze on the sofa in front of the television. Now that the baby was getting really big, she was tired a lot of the time. Dad and Evie always took a ball with them, or Leo's favorite, a rubber disk. Dad had seen it in the pet store and bought it for when Leo was bigger, but once Leo saw it, he didn't want to wait. So what if the disk was almost as big as he was? He was very good at catching it — he could do massive leaps in midair, twisting and turning and snatching the disk as it fell. Then he'd haul it over the grass back to Evie, and sit panting exhaustedly for a minute, before yapping for them to throw it again. A couple of times he'd worn himself out so much that Dad had to carry him home and lay the exhausted puppy in his basket. Evie was so happy that Leo had become part of the family — she couldn't imagine life at home without him now.

Chapter Three

One night, Leo was curled up snugly in a nest of comforter on top of Evie's toes. He was twitching happily in his sleep, dreaming of breakfast, when he was woken by the sound of Evie's parents talking. He sat up and listened carefully — it wasn't something he expected to hear in the middle of the night. Something interesting was going on. He padded up to the top of the bed, and licked Evie's ear.

"Grrmmpf!" Evie wriggled and wiped the drool off her face. "Leo! It's the middle of the night, silly. What are you doing?" She yawned, and gave a little stretch. "Go back to sleep. It's a long time until we have to get up." Then she turned over and snuggled her face back into her pillow.

Leo huffed through his nose irritably. Why wouldn't Evie listen? Couldn't she tell that something exciting was happening? He grabbed Evie's pajama sleeve with his teeth, very, very gently, and pulled.

"Okay, Leo, what is it?" she asked sleepily. "Do you need to go to the bathroom? Because if you think I'm taking you all around the yard to find a good place at this time of night you can think again!"

Leo yapped sharply, and tugged at Evie's sleeve again. Then he dropped the sleeve and stood silently, his ears pricked up.

Evie listened, and at last she understood why Leo was behaving so strangely. Her parents weren't just talking now, they were moving around, too. Doors were opening and shutting quietly, and she could hear her dad on the phone to someone, sounding anxious. The baby was coming! It had to be that. Evie pulled her pillow up and leaned back against it, whispering to Leo to come and sit with her. He burrowed in under her arm and they listened together in the dark. Someone was arriving downstairs.

"That'll be Grandma, I bet," Evie whispered. "They said they'd ask her to come and stay with me when they had to go to the hospital."

Leo grunted in agreement. He liked

Grandma. She had dog treats in her purse.

A few minutes later, the front door banged, and they heard someone coming back up the stairs. At last Evie's bedroom door eased open, and Grandma poked her head around.

"Hi, Grandma!" Evie whispered.

"Hello, darling! I thought you might have woken up, with all the coming and going. I just came to check on you."

"Leo woke me up. Is Mom having the baby now?" Evie sounded anxious.

Grandma perched herself on the end of Evie's bed, and petted Leo's nose.

"Clever Leo. Yes, they think so. Don't get too excited, though — these things can take a while." She smiled down at Evie, still cuddling the little dog, and decided that she'd been wrong to worry. Evie loved him so much, and a dog would be just what her granddaughter needed to keep her company over the next few weeks.

The next day Evie's parents brought baby Sam home. Evie's mom and Sam were both doing really well, and they didn't need to stay in the hospital. Mom said the noise of all the other babies in the hospital was driving her insane, and she wanted to be home in her own bed.

Even though they were coming home as soon as they possibly could, the wait still seemed like forever to Evie. It was a Saturday, so she was home, with Leo and Grandma. The day really dragged, even though as a treat they all walked to a nearby restaurant to get lunch. Grandma stood outside with Leo, who was blissfully breathing in the smell of fries, and Evie went in to get their food. When they got back, both Evie and Grandma naughtily fed Leo the odd fry under the table, so he was soon full and fast asleep.

Evie couldn't help listening for the car — Dad had called to say they'd be home sometime that afternoon, and they just had to wait for the doctor to give Mom one last check. Their road was pretty quiet, but Evie ran to the window to look at least ten times before she finally spotted their car pulling up.

"They're here!" she squeaked. Grandma came hurrying over to join Evie.

Evie's dad was trying to get the new baby seat out of the car and all they could see of her new brother was a little bit of blue blanket trailing out of the seat.

Leo couldn't tell what Evie was thinking, which was odd, because usually he had a good idea. Was she happy about this strange new thing that was happening? He licked her hand, and made a questioning little "wuff?" noise.

"That's the baby, Leo. My brother, Sam. Let's go and see." Evie scrambled down from the windowsill, and Leo trotted after her out into the hallway. Grandma had opened the door, and Evie's parents were just bringing the baby in.

"Evie!" Mom hugged her tightly.

"I missed you. Were you and Grandma okay?"

"Of course. Can I see him, Mom?" Evie crouched down next to the baby seat and peered in. Sam seemed tiny inside — just a small hand clenched tightly around the blanket, and a pale little face half-covered by a hat.

"Let's get him in and unwrap him, then you can see him. It's a little chilly outside so he had to be covered up," Mom explained.

Leo followed interestedly as the family went into the kitchen. The baby smelled new and different, and he wanted to investigate.

Grandma and Evie watched as Mom unzipped Sam's little jacket, with Dad's help. At last she stood up, and carried him over. "Do you want to sit down, Evie?" she asked. "Then you can hold him."

Evie whisked over to a chair and sat down, eagerly holding out her arms.

Mom kissed Sam's nose, and handed him very carefully to Evie. "Sam, this is your big sister!"

Evie sat holding Sam, a look of amazement on her face. "He's smaller than some of my old dolls," she whispered, looking worriedly up at Mom. "Is he all right?"

Dad laughed. "He'll grow. You were smaller than that."

Evie gazed down at Sam, watching as his eyes gradually opened. "He's looking right at me!" she squealed, beaming in delight.

Mom laughed. "I think he is! They say new babies can't really see much, but he's definitely staring at you."

"You know, he looks a lot like Evie," Dad put in.

"Yes, I see what you mean," Grandma agreed.

Leo watched as they all chattered excitedly. He was feeling confused. No one had introduced him to the new baby. Evie was his person, and she was ignoring him. He gave a sharp little yap, and everyone jumped. The tiny creature on Evie's lap gasped and let out a shuddering wail that made Leo back away. What was it?

"Leo!" Evie said angrily. "What did you do that for? Look, you've made Sam cry."

Leo backed away even further, his tail tucked between his legs. Now Evie was angry with him. He wasn't sure he liked this *baby* thing at all.

Over the next few days, Evie fell in love with her new little brother. Sam didn't do much, except lie in a bassinet and wail occasionally, but he was very cute. Evie's dad had some time off work to help out, so Evie had tried arguing that she ought to have time off from school, too, but apparently it didn't work that way. She had to go back to school on Monday morning. Dad dropped her off in the car.

"You will bring Sam to pick me up, won't you?" she begged her mom. "I want everyone to see him. He's so much nicer than anyone else's little brothers and sisters."

The trip to pick up Evie from school was the first time Mom had taken Sam out in his new stroller. Leo watched as Dad wrestled with the stroller. It would be nice to take a walk. He'd been let out in the yard over the weekend, but no one had taken him for a proper run, and he was anxious to be out smelling some good smells. Leo went to fetch his leash — it hung over a hook in the hall, and he could tug it down. He trotted back with it in his mouth just as Mom was maneuvering the stroller over the front step.

"You're sure you don't want me to come?" Dad asked again.

"No, you start making the tea; we'll be fine." And she closed the door behind her. Without Leo!

Leo barked to remind Mom she'd left him behind — it wasn't like her to forget, but maybe that baby had distracted her.

"Not today, Leo." Dad shook his head. "Sorry, boy, but it's a bit much to have you *and* the stroller." He patted Leo's head and went back into the kitchen, leaving Leo in the hall, his leash still trailing out of his mouth.

Leo stared at the door, confused. He always went to pick Evie up from school. Was Evie's mom really not coming back for him?

"Leo! Treat!"

Evie's dad was calling. Leo gave the door one last hopeful look. Oh, well. He supposed a treat was better than nothing....

When Mom and Evie got back from school, they were both looking a bit frazzled. Sam had snoozed most of the way, and then woken up just in time for everyone to say how cute he was, but now he was hungry, and upset, and a loud wailing noise was coming from his nest of blankets.

Mom sat on the sofa to feed him, and Evie curled up next to her to watch — she'd really missed seeing Sam while she was at school. Leo jumped up, too — he thought they were going to watch television together, like they usually did. But Evie squeaked in horror and pushed him off. "Leo, no! You might squash Sam!"

Leo's tail drooped, and he slunk miserably into the kitchen. The baby was going to watch all his favorite shows with Evie instead. It wasn't fair.

All the next week, people kept stopping by with presents for the new baby, and quite often one for Evie, too. Everyone seemed to think Sam was very special, and he got fussed over all the time. Leo wasn't quite sure why. Sam didn't do a lot, and he certainly couldn't do tricks like a dog could. Leo couldn't help wishing that things would go back to normal, and everyone would fuss over him instead, but he had a feeling it wasn't going to happen.

But at least Leo had been able to reclaim his place on the sofa, as Mom said she thought it was okay for Leo to sit there when she was feeding Sam, as long as Evie was careful not to let Leo lick him.

"Leo's used to sitting there with you, Evie," she pointed out. "It isn't fair if he's not allowed to anymore. Just keep an eye on him." She sat Sam up to get him to burp, and smiled. "Look, Sam's watching Leo's tail wag. I think he'll love having Leo for company."

Evie scratched Leo behind the ears, and he settled down on her lap, keeping a watchful eye on the baby. He supposed he didn't mind sharing the sofa.

Chapter Four

"Evie! Evie! You're going to be late for school!" Mom was calling up the stairs, sounding angry. She had Sam tucked under one arm, and he was crying. "You won't have time for breakfast!"

Evie stomped down the stairs looking very gloomy. "I don't want any. And I don't want to go to school, either. I don't feel very well. I'm really tired."

Evie's mom took a deep breath and counted to five. "I know. We all are. But it's Friday, and you can sleep in over the weekend."

"If Sam doesn't keep me awake all night, like he did last night," Evie growled.

"It's not his fault, Evie. He doesn't understand the difference between night and day yet." Mom was sounding really exhausted.

"Well, can't you teach him?" Evie looked up at her mom and suddenly grinned. "Oh, all right. I guess not. But I am really, really tired." She sighed and hooked her finger into Sam's tiny hand. "Don't you dare nap all afternoon, Sam. Stay up and then you'll sleep tonight!"

It hadn't been a good week. Evie's dad was back at work now, and it was harder to get everything done without the extra help. Sam was beautiful, but he wasn't sleeping well, and when he was awake he was loud. Everyone's temper was flaring.

Leo was trying his best to keep out of the way, but he never managed to be in the right place. Most days Evie's mom walked into him about three times just doing the laundry. When she got back from taking Evie to school that Friday, she tripped over Leo while she was carrying a basket of laundry, and stepped on his paw, but she didn't seem to be sorry. He held it up and whined, but all she did was snap, "Leo! Not again! Get out of the way, you silly dog!" Leo limped out of the kitchen, feeling very upset.

He sat in the hallway, thoughtfully chewing on a small teddy bear he'd found on the stairs. He just couldn't seem to do anything right anymore. Things had been much nicer before.

At that moment, Sam started crying upstairs and Mom dashed past to go and get him — and saw the small pile of shredded fur that had once been a teddy bear. "Leo!" she wailed, and 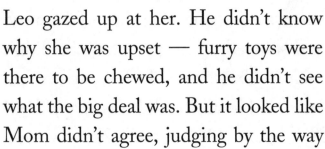 Leo gazed up at her. He didn't know why she was upset — furry toys were there to be chewed, and he didn't see what the big deal was. But it looked like Mom didn't agree, judging by the way she snatched up what was left of the teddy bear and glared at him.

Leo was still moping when Grandma came by that afternoon, and he was delighted to see her. At last someone who actually had time to sit and scratch him behind the ears properly! He leaned against Grandma's leg affectionately. For a moment he almost wished that she would take him back to her house. Then he shook his head and snorted. No! He was Evie's dog. He was sure that she would get over the baby thing soon, and then maybe they could go back to taking walks and more cuddling.

"You look exhausted!" Grandma was saying to Mom. "Why don't you go upstairs and take a nap? I'll take care of

Sam for you."

Mom sighed. "I'd love to, but he's being so grumpy today. He wouldn't even go to his dad this morning — every time I put him down he howls. I just don't know what's the matter with him. Anyway, I've got to go and get Evie in a minute."

Grandma stood up firmly. "Put him in the stroller and I'll take him with me and get Evie for you. You go and rest. Sam will probably sleep, too."

"If you're sure…." Mom tucked Sam in and set off upstairs, looking grateful.

Me, too! Me, too! Leo whined hopefully, bouncing around Grandma's ankles as she headed for the door. He was still desperate for more walks.

"Sorry, Leo. I'd love to take you,

but I'm not used to this stroller and I can't manage both of you." She looked down at the little dog thoughtfully. "I'd better talk to Evie about you. I don't think she's exercising you enough."

Leo yelped in agreement, and she nodded to herself.

Unfortunately, Grandma's master plan for settling Sam didn't work. At five o'clock, when she had to leave to go home to feed Tigger and Ben, Sam was still wailing. And when Evie's dad walked in at six, he was greeted by a howling baby, a frazzled wife, and an angry daughter.

"Looks like we're in for a fun weekend," he joked, but no one else thought it was funny.

Leo watched Dad hopefully. Mom and Evie had been so stressed by Sam's crying that they had forgotten to feed him. He nosed eagerly at his food bowl, and looked up at Dad. He wasn't watching. Leo sighed and trailed back to his basket, where he curled up with his back to the rest of the family. Maybe he'd better just sleep and try again in a little while.

A couple of hours later, Leo was convinced he was going to starve if he didn't get fed soon. He trotted into the living room, where Mom and Dad were taking turns walking with Sam. Evie was just getting ready to go up to bed. Leo was horrified. If Evie went to bed, they'd never remember to feed him! Desperate measures were needed. He scurried back to the kitchen.

"Oh, thank goodness," Mom whispered, watching as Sam slumped slightly on his dad's shoulder. "He's going to sleep. No, don't stop!"

Dad nodded grimly, and resumed his trek around the room. "I think he's fallen asleep," he sighed, a couple of minutes later. "Can we risk lying him down, do you—"

It was at that moment that Leo trotted back in, carrying his metal food bowl in his teeth. He dropped it hard on the wooden floor and barked.

Sam shot upright and let out a bloodcurdling wail.

"Leo! You bad dog!" Mom groaned. "That's it. Kitchen! Now! In your basket!" And she shooed him out, waving her hands angrily.

Leo was banished. It was the first night he'd ever spent in the kitchen, instead of curled up on the end of Evie's bed. He was so confused. He'd only wanted to eat! Everyone else had eaten, and he was starving.

For the next hour, Leo and Sam howled together. Then Sam suddenly decided not to bother anymore and fell blissfully asleep; but Leo lay in his basket, and stared at the dark kitchen. Why didn't Evie want him upstairs? What had he done?

Didn't she love him anymore?

Chapter Five

The next morning was Saturday, and the family was having breakfast. It was always a really nice time — the beginning of the weekend, when they all had a chance to relax. They usually had something extra-nice for breakfast, too. Today, not even croissants could cheer everyone up.

At least Sam seemed to be in a better

mood. He was lying in his bouncy chair in the living room.

"He's fine," Dad reported back after a quick check. "Seems to be enjoying himself, actually — I think he's learning to bat at that toy you bought him, Evie." He gave a long, slow sigh of relief, and sat down and poured himself a large cup of coffee.

Leo jumped up, his paws on Dad's knee, holding his squeaky bone hopefully in his mouth. Dad was usually good for a game.

"Not now, Leo," Dad muttered, pushing him away gently.

Leo went to paw at Evie's ankles, hoping for a bit of croissant. She dangled a piece by his nose, and he gulped it down gratefully.

"Evie!" Mom said sharply. "Are you giving Leo scraps? How many times have I told you not to feed that dog at the table?" Mom didn't normally mind that much, but today she was tired and cranky.

"Shoo, Leo!" Evie whispered, nudging him out from under the table with her foot.

Leo took one look at Mom's angry face, and trailed sadly into the living room. He sat down next to Sam. The baby was half-smiling at the bouncy animals toy stretched across the front of his chair, and vaguely waving a hand at it every so often. Leo watched. It was fun. He lay down with his nose on his paws and gazed up as the little creatures jumped and danced.

Sam smelled nice — milky — and he was relaxing to be with after the tense, grumpy mood in the kitchen. Sam made little squeaky, grunting noises to himself, and Leo woofed quietly back, his eyes slowly closing as he drifted off for a snooze.

After a few minutes, the jingling of the toy was joined by an irritating buzz. Leo opened one eye. Was it Sam making that noise? Was he supposed to do that? No, Sam was asleep. The buzzing was from a large fly that had landed on the baby's arm. Leo bristled as he watched it crawl over Sam. He hated flies, and he knew Evie's mom did, too; if a fly buzzed nearby, she always shooed it away. That fly should *not* be crawling over Sam.

Leo watched, waiting for his moment to pounce. He was so intent on the fly that he had no idea Evie and her mom had come into the living room to check on Sam. They watched in horror as Leo pounced, his sharp white teeth snapping on the fly — just inches away from Sam's arm.

"Leo, no!" Evie screamed, as her mom threw herself forward to grab Sam away.

Leo had never heard Evie sound like that before — terrified and angry at the same time. He shot under the sofa and lay there, cowering.

Sam hadn't noticed the fly, but he certainly noticed when his mom snatched him out of his sleep. He roared angrily, and waved his arms around.

"Mom, is he okay? I can't believe Leo tried to bite him!" Tears were rolling down Evie's cheeks.

Evie's mom was breathing fast — from where she and Evie had been standing, it really had looked as though Leo had meant to bite Sam's arm, and she'd been terrified. She was pushing up the sleeve of his pajamas, searching for marks, but he seemed fine — just upset at being woken.

"What happened? Are you all right?" Evie's dad rushed into the room, his robe flapping. "Is something wrong with Sam?" he asked, taking in the scene.

"No. No, we're all okay," Evie's mom said slowly.

"Dad, Leo almost bit Sam!" Evie sobbed, throwing her arms around him. She couldn't believe that her sweet puppy would do such an awful thing — but then she'd seen it with her own eyes and watched him jump at her baby brother, teeth bared.

"I don't think he did, Evie." Mom sounded as though she were trying to figure it all out. "Look."

Lying on the floor next to the bouncy chair was a huge fly, legs in the air, still buzzing faintly.

"You know how Leo hates flies. He's always snapping at them. I think he just tried to catch a fly that had landed on Sam's arm."

Evie lifted her head from where it was buried in her dad's robe. "Really?"

Evie's dad was looking serious. "Are you sure?"

"Well, no, I suppose not. But Leo's never done anything like that before, has he?"

Evie shook her head, smiling in relief. "Never! Oh, Mom, thank goodness you saw that fly — we'd never have known otherwise."

"Where is Leo?" Dad asked, looking around.

"I shouted at him and he disappeared under the sofa!" Evie went pale. "Oh, he must think we're so angry! Poor Leo." Evie crouched down to look, but Leo flinched away from her, and retreated to the back. Evie sat up, looking hurt. "He won't come," she said miserably.

"You probably need to give him some time." Dad put an arm around her, and the other around Mom and Sam. "Come on into the kitchen."

Leo huddled under the sofa, trembling. No one had ever shouted at him like

79

that before. Evie had behaved as though he'd done something terrible. But he'd been helping Sam! Evie's mom was always saying that flies were horrible, dirty things. She waved them away if they got anywhere near the baby. *Did Evie and Mom think I was trying to bite Sam?* Leo wondered. *I'd never do that! Don't they know I'd never do that?* Leo lay there, feeling confused. No one seemed to understand him very much here anymore. He was always in trouble, and even Evie, who used to love him so much, didn't seem to have any time for him. Maybe they really did think he was the kind of dog who would bite.

"Leo! Leo!" Evie was calling him. She was lying down, peering under the sofa.

"Come out, Leo, please? I didn't mean it. Please come out. I'm so sorry for shouting at you." Her eyes met his hopefully, and Leo couldn't hold back any longer.

He crept forward, tail slowly starting to wag. As he wriggled out from under the sofa, she hugged him tight, burying her face in his thick white fur. "Oh, Leo." Leo put his paws on her shoulders and licked her face, tasting salt from her tears. Why was she crying? Everything was all right now. He wagged his tail, and licked her again lovingly.

"Ugh, Leo...." Evie giggled and sniffed. "I'm covered in dog drool. Oh, I do love you." She sighed. "I'm so sorry. I haven't been showing it much, have I?"

Leo woofed encouragingly. He adored Evie, and he trusted her. Hearing the love in Evie's voice as he snuggled against her was all he needed to feel better.

Chapter Six

The rest of the day was almost perfect for Leo. Evie seemed to be back to her old self. She cuddled him a lot, and she kept saying she was sorry for thinking he'd hurt Sam, and telling him what a clever dog he was for catching the fly. Just every so often, Leo would remember how upset and angry everyone had been, and shudder, and then Evie would hug him all over again.

Only one thing spoiled it. Leo kept catching worried looks between Evie's mom and dad — worried looks directed at him. Maybe they thought he might still be frightened. He tried to be extra bouncy and friendly, with lots of jumping up to lick them, but it didn't seem to work. If anything, they looked more worried, although they always patted him and smiled.

Evie gave him a huge meal and Leo was so full afterward that he went to sleep on her lap while she was trying to finish her homework at the kitchen table. He didn't notice Evie's parents coming to sit with her, or see the anxious looks on their faces.

"Evie." Mom sounded strangely nervous. "Evie, we have to talk to you, sweetheart."

Evie looked up. "I'm doing it! Look, I'm doing it now. It's only Saturday, Mom. I'll get it done, easily!"

"Not about your homework." Dad's voice was really flat, and Evie looked at him, suddenly scared. This was far more serious than just them complaining that she was rushing through her homework at the last minute.

"It's about Leo," Dad went on.

Her heart suddenly thumping, Evie put her hand down to pet Leo, curled up on her lap. He gave a little whine of pleasure, and stretched out luxuriously in his sleep before curling himself up again even tighter. "What's the matter?" Evie asked quietly.

Her mom and dad exchanged a look, then her dad sighed. "We're not sure we can keep him, Evie."

Evie gulped, her hand tightening on Leo's neck so that he wriggled uncomfortably. "Why?" she whispered. Then her voice strengthened. "He wasn't biting, Dad, really," she assured him. "He wouldn't do that." She smiled desperately at her dad, knowing she had to convince him.

"Evie, you thought he would," Dad said gently. "And so did your mom. You were so upset this morning."

"But he didn't! It was all a mistake." Evie's eyes were filling with tears. Her dad sounded so set in the decision. She turned to her mom for help, and saw that she was crying, too.

"It's not Leo's fault at all. It's just that we haven't been able to take care of Leo properly, Evie," her mom said shakily. "We all love him, but he needs walks, and lots of attention. He hasn't been getting that. Dogs can get very grumpy if they're cooped up in the house all day."

"I'll walk him more!" Evie cried out. "Every day! Twice a day. I've just been busy with having Sam around, that's all."

"We all have," her dad agreed. "But that's not fair to Leo — he needs a home where he doesn't get forgotten about."

"I didn't mean to!" Evie wailed, so loudly that Leo woke up, his little white head suddenly popping up at the table, making them all giggle hopelessly.

He gave them a happy smile, showing lots of long pink tongue. What was the joke? Then he looked again, turning to sniff at Evie. Maybe there wasn't a joke at all. Something felt wrong. Had he done something bad again? He hunched down onto Evie's lap, looking scared.

"Evie, look at him. He's upset. It's not fair to put him through that," Evie's mom said gently.

Evie sniffed. "If — if we're not going to keep him, what are we going to do? Are you going to give him back to Mrs. Wilson?" She gulped, imagining Leo sitting sadly in the puppy room all on his own, his brother and sisters already gone to new homes.

"No." Dad looked thoughtful. "It would have been the best option, but she's stopped breeding dogs now. She's retired to the seaside, remember?"

"I suppose she might take just Leo back…," Mom said. "Oh, but we don't have her new address."

"I think the sensible thing would be to take him to the animal shelter," Dad said firmly, as though he were trying to convince himself.

"The animal shelter?" Evie's eyes filled with tears again. "Where Grandma got Ben and Tigger? But that's for dogs that people don't want! We *do* want Leo!"

"Dogs that people can't keep, Evie." Mom's voice sounded so sorry that Evie knew there was no point in arguing. Hugging Leo to her, she jumped up and raced up the stairs to her room.

Evie didn't come down for dinner. Leo had already had a huge meal, and he was delighted to stay upstairs with Evie all evening. She was giving him lots of attention, teasing and tickling him, and playing all his favorite games. At bedtime he was allowed to snuggle up on her bed again. Leo heaved a deep, happy sigh. This was where he was meant to be, not down in the kitchen on his own. Everything was the way it should be. He fell asleep at once, worn out from all the playing — so he didn't notice that Evie lay awake half the night, tears rolling silently down her cheeks.

"Evie, you don't have to come."

Leo looked interestedly back and forth between Evie and Dad. They were going somewhere! He padded off to get his leash, and jumped up with his paws on Evie's knees to give it to her.

Evie gulped, and tears started to seep from the corners of her eyes again. He was such a wonderful dog! How could they be doing this? Hurriedly she wiped the tears away — she didn't want Leo to know what was going on. "I'm coming," she said firmly, her voice hardly shaking at all. "I don't want Leo to think I didn't say good-bye."

Dad sighed. "Okay. Hey, Leo, come on, boy. You're going for a car ride," he said, trying to sound cheerful.

But Leo laid his ears back. Something odd was going on. He jumped into the car and saw that Evie's hands were trembling as she fastened his harness. Usually Evie would beg her dad to have the radio on and they'd sing along, but today they hardly spoke at all.

When the car stopped, Leo thought Evie would put his leash on and let him walk, but for some reason she was carrying him up in front of her so she could nuzzle into his fur. Leo licked her face gratefully. He liked being carried, so he could see what was going on. Evie was walking very slowly, though — Dad kept stopping and looking back for her as they headed toward the building. Leo wasn't surprised. It didn't smell good, too clean, a little like the vet's that he'd been taken to a few weeks before.

What was this place?

Evie stood by the reception desk, while Dad explained quietly to a girl in a green uniform. She was nodding sympathetically, and she gave Leo a considering look.

"I'm sure he'll find a new home very quickly. He's a beautiful little dog." She came around the reception desk and held out her arms. "Come on, sweetie," she crooned to Leo.

Leo felt suddenly scared. Who was this girl? Why were they here? All at once he knew that the wonderful, cuddly time he'd been having with Evie over the last day hadn't been real. In fact, nothing had been right since he'd snapped at that fly on Sam's arm. But he still didn't understand! What should he have done? He scrambled helplessly as the girl in green lifted him from Evie's arms. He was squealing with fright, desperately trying to get away.

"Come on, Evie." Her dad quickly marched Evie away, before she grabbed Leo back again. Leo's last sight of Evie was as her dad hustled her out the door, hugging her tightly against him, so that she couldn't turn and see her little dog howling for her to come back.

Chapter Seven

As Evie trailed up the front path, she heard someone calling her, and excited woofs. She spun around immediately, thinking that somehow it was Leo.

"Hello, Evie! Ben and Tigger and I are just out for our walk. We thought we'd see if you and Leo wanted to come with us. I know you haven't had a lot of time to walk him lately."

Grandma was beaming at Evie, but then she noticed Evie's dad, who was shaking his head and holding his finger to lips.

"Jack, are you all right?" Grandma asked worriedly, as Tigger and Ben towed her through the gate.

Evie's dad sighed. "Not really."

Evie crouched down to pat Ben and Tigger. "We just took Leo to the animal shelter," she told them quietly. Somehow it was easier to tell the dogs than Grandma. Suddenly she remembered. "You were right, Grandma. You said we wouldn't be able to manage."

"Oh, sweetheart, I'm really sorry." Grandma's face crumpled. "I hadn't realized it was that bad. Why didn't you say something?" she asked Evie's dad.

He shrugged. "It was one of those difficult decisions…," he said sadly. "I'm sure someone really nice will take Leo home. You know that, Evie, don't you?"

Evie was fighting back tears. She didn't want anybody else taking Leo anywhere, even if they fed him out of a solid gold bowl! He was her dog — only he wasn't. Not anymore. In fact, she suddenly realized, she was never going to see him again. She gasped, and then she scrambled up and dashed into the house, tears stinging her eyes.

"That little Westie's still not eating."

"Really? He's only been here three days. He'll change his mind soon."

The two girls in the green uniforms at the animal shelter leaned against the wall, sipping their tea, and staring thoughtfully into Leo's cage. He was curled up at the back, a miserable little ball, not even looking at his overflowing food bowl.

"He's really taking it hard, poor little thing."

"Yeah, I was here when they brought him in — the little girl he belonged to was really upset, too."

Leo snuggled his paws further around his ears to shut out their voices. If he kept his eyes shut tight, he could almost pretend that he was back home.

"Leo! Leo!"

Leo twitched, but it wasn't Evie. It was another of the animal shelter staff, with some people looking for a dog. Quite a few people had been to see Leo already, and everyone said how cute he was. They seemed surprised, as though such a sweet puppy shouldn't really be at a place like this. But when they tried to talk to Leo, and he refused to budge from the back of his cage, they gave up, moving on to friendlier dogs.

"Mom, look at this great dog!" A boy about Evie's age was peering through the cage. "Can we meet him? Please?"

"Sure." One of the girls who worked at the animal shelter got out her keys. "This is Leo. He's a beautiful Westie puppy who needs a new home because his owners had a baby and couldn't keep him. He's a sweet boy, but he's not too happy right now. Hey, Leo…," she cooed gently to him. "Come and meet Ethan. He's looking for a nice dog just like you."

Leo hunched himself up tighter. The staff at the shelter were right. He hadn't accepted what was going on. How could he? He didn't understand. He couldn't let anyone take him home, because Evie was coming back for him. He was sure of it. But he was becoming just a little less sure every time he woke up and he was still in a gray concrete cage, waiting for her.

The girl picked him up, and Leo lay limply and sadly in her arms as she carried him out. The little boy petted him gently. "He's great."

Ethan's eyes were shining, just like Evie's used to. Leo let Ethan scratch him behind the ears. That was nice.

"Can we take him home?" Ethan begged.

Home! Leo suddenly twisted in the girl's arms, and growled angrily. What was he thinking? His home was with Evie.

Ethan's parents pulled him away quickly to look at another dog, and the girl with the keys sighed. "Oh, Leo. That would have been a wonderful home. When are you going to let someone else love you?"

Leo slunk back into his cage and curled up facing the wall. He only wanted *Evie* to love him.

Evie thought it was strange that her house could feel so different, just because Leo wasn't there. She didn't have a warm body curled on her toes at night. No cold nose was resting on her knee at mealtimes, hoping for scraps. Only Mom and Sam met her at school, and she and Dad didn't go for walks anymore. Leo's leaving had changed everything.

She tried to explain to Grandma when she went to her house after school on Wednesday.

"I never realized how nice it was having Leo to play with when Mom was busy. She's got so much to do with feeding Sam, and everything. But I had Leo, and it was okay. I really miss him, Grandma." She stared into her juice, and Tigger pushed his head into her lap, sensing that she was unhappy. "Yeah, you miss him, too, don't you, Tigger?"

"I should think your parents miss Leo as well, you know," Grandma said.

Evie nodded miserably. "I think Dad does. I caught him in the hall yesterday with Leo's leash. He looked really confused, and he muttered something about having forgotten. We sometimes used to take Leo for walks after dinner."

"Why don't you talk to them about it? You might have made the wrong decision." Grandma looked thoughtfully at Evie, wondering what she'd say.

Evie petted Tigger. Then she looked up, and her face was so sad that Grandma caught her breath. "I shouldn't ever have let him go, Grandma!" She got up to put on her coat. "I miss Leo so much."

Grandma nodded firmly. "I definitely think you should talk to them." She watched Evie walking slowly down the path, and then looked down at Ben and Tigger. They stared back at her encouragingly. "Mmm. Yes, I think you're right," Grandma muttered to herself.

A couple of times during the week, Evie thought about what Grandma had said, but there didn't seem any point in talking to Mom and Dad about Leo. It would just make everything worse when they said no, and she was sure she wouldn't change their minds. Then on Saturday morning she wandered into the kitchen and found her mom staring at something on the table with a funny look on her face.

"What's the matter?" Evie leaned over to see what she was looking at, and saw that her mom was holding a photo of Leo.

"Oh! Evie, I didn't hear you come in." Mom quickly put the photo back on the windowsill, but Evie was staring at her.

"You miss him, too, don't you?" she asked, her voice suddenly full of hope. "Grandma said you did, but I didn't believe her." Then her shoulders slumped. "But I suppose it doesn't make any difference." She looked over at Sam, who was sitting in his bouncy chair staring in wonder at his toes. She still adored her baby brother, but she couldn't help thinking that it was his fault.

Mom looked, too. "Maybe." Then her voice changed. "Maybe not, Evie. Maybe we were being too hard on him."

"Who?" Dad walked in with the newspaper. "Got you some chocolate, Evie," he added, throwing her a bar.

Evie caught it, but didn't even look to see what kind it was. "Dad, Mom thinks maybe we shouldn't have taken

Leo to the animal shelter!"

Her dad sat down at the table slowly, looking back and forth between them. "Really?" he said thoughtfully.

Mom sat down, too. "Come on. Tell me you haven't missed him."

"But that's not the point! We weren't able to take care of him properly. And what about Sam? Think back to this time last week!"

"I think we overreacted. We panicked — we were all tired, and we made a snap decision. I don't think it was a good one." Mom reached out for his hand. "Leo was such fun to have around. Do you really think he would have hurt Sam?"

Evie watched hopefully, holding her breath as Dad shook his head. "To be honest, I think watching Leo cheered the little guy up sometimes," he said.

They looked over at Sam, who stared back seriously, and said, "Ooooo" in a meaningful way, waving his foot.

"And I really missed taking him to the newsstand this morning," Dad added. "You know, I never came out of the store and found Leo on his own — he was always being petted by someone. Everyone loved him."

Evie took a deep breath. "So can we go and get him back?" she asked, twisting her fingers together anxiously.

Dad looked serious. "It wasn't just about Sam, though, Evie. We'd need to take care of Leo better." He exchanged a glance with Mom. "We need to think this through."

Mom nodded. "Evie, could you do me a big favor and change Sam's diaper?"

"Now?" Evie asked disbelievingly.

"Yes, now." Mom smiled at her. "Your dad and I need to talk. And Sam needs a diaper change."

Evie picked Sam up, making a face, and carried him upstairs.

When Evie got back, Mom and Dad were looking at the photo of Leo again. "Have you decided?" Evie asked hopefully, cuddling Sam close.

"Do you think we can all be better owners for Leo this time around?" Dad asked.

"Yes! And Grandma would help!" Evie reminded him. "She said she would. I could take him out for walks with her and Ben and Tigger."

"No getting grumpy with Leo just because Sam has made us tired."

"No! I promise. Pleeease! Can we have him back?"

Dad grinned at her. "Okay. Let's go and get Leo!"

Evie and her parents were talking excitedly in the car about how great it was going to be to have Leo back, when Dad suddenly stopped in the middle of his favorite story about Leo trying to catch a pigeon.

"I just thought about something," he said quietly. "It's possible someone else has already given Leo a new home. He's been at the shelter a week — and he's such a beautiful dog. Evie, I don't want to upset you, but it's possible Leo's gone."

Evie gulped. "Can you drive faster?"

Evie and her dad jumped out of the car as soon as they got to the animal shelter, while Mom wrestled with Sam and the stroller. "You go!" she said, waving them on.

They dashed into the waiting area, and Dad explained why they had come back, while Evie hopped up and down impatiently. The girl at the desk was taking so long to bring up Leo's file on the computer. At last Evie couldn't stand it. She slipped through the big double door that led to the cages. She had to tell Leo he was coming home!

But Leo wasn't there.

Chapter Eight

"And they wouldn't tell you who'd taken him?" Mom asked indignantly.

"Well, no. I can see why not. We gave Leo up. It wouldn't be fair on his new owners if we could just storm over there and take him back," Dad pointed out.

Mom sighed. "I suppose not. But it seems so unfair."

"Can we not talk about it?" came a small voice from the backseat. Evie was sadly dangling a toy in front of Sam's carseat, and he was giggling, the only member of the family feeling cheerful.

"Sorry, Evie. You're right. It's not going to change anything. At least we're going to Grandma's for lunch — that'll make us feel better. I'll bet she's made a cake."

Evie stared at the car ceiling, concentrating on not snapping at her parents. They were only trying to be nice — but honestly, a cake? That was supposed to make it all right that she'd just lost her beautiful dog forever? Evie sniffed hard. She didn't want to start crying again. She'd finally managed to stop, and her eyes were hurting. She adored Grandma, but she wished they weren't going to her house today. Grandma would never have let anything like this happen to Ben or Tigger, and seeing them was just going to make Evie miss Leo more.

He'll be with a wonderful family, she told herself firmly. He'll be having a great time. The people at the animal shelter wouldn't give him to anyone who wouldn't take care of him well. Someone like us, she couldn't help adding.

Evie had never noticed how many dogs lived in the few streets between her house and Grandma's, but that afternoon they seemed to be everywhere. As they turned the corner onto Grandma's road, she could hear excited yapping, and something tugged in her stomach. It sounded just like Leo. But it was only Ben and Tigger, playing in the front yard. Grandma let them out there sometimes for a change.

Dad put his arm around Evie's shoulders. "You can still come and play with these two, you know," he said sympathetically.

Evie nodded. But it wasn't the same as having her own dog. Although she'd never noticed before how much Ben sounded like Leo. It was weird that he had that same squeaky bark. Actually, he probably didn't — she was just going to imagine Leo everywhere for a while. *I wonder how long that will last?* Evie thought to herself miserably. *Forever, I suppose.* She leaned over the gate to undo the latch and the dogs bounded over to say hello.

All three of them.

"Leo!" Evie gasped, finally realizing that the squeaky bark sounded like Leo because it *was* Leo. It was Leo jumping twice his own height to try to get over the gate to greet her. "Leo!" She fought with the latch, but she was crying so much that Dad had to open it for her. Leo shot into her arms and tried to lick her all over, his woofs getting squeakier than ever with excitement.

You came back! You came back! he was saying delightedly, if Evie could have understood him.

"I don't understand," Evie said dazedly, as they sat at the kitchen table. Mom had been right. There was a delicious-looking cake, although at the moment only Leo seemed interested in it. He was perched on Evie's knee, gradually easing himself closer and closer to one of the delicious bits.

Grandma smiled. "Well, after I talked to you, Evie, I changed my mind. I hadn't thought you were ready to have a dog — it's such a huge responsibility. But then with Leo gone, you seemed so sad. And I love Leo, too. I decided that even if you didn't feel you could have him back right now, with Sam so little, then I would keep him myself and you could visit him. Ben and Tigger like having a bouncy young dog to cheer them up." She looked over at her dogs, who were slumped exhaustedly on their cushions, and smiled. Tigger seemed to have his paws over his eyes. "Mmmm. Well, the extra exercise is good for them."

"We can take him home, can't we? He can live with us, like Grandma said. And Grandma can help us out if we're having a problem?" Evie asked her parents anxiously.

"Definitely!" said her dad. "Leo's part of the family. Aren't you, boy?" Then he laughed. "And Sam thinks so, too."

Sam was sitting on Mom's lap, next to Evie and Leo. He was leaning over toward Leo, his fingers clumsily batting at Leo's shiny collar tag, so that it jingled and flashed in the sun. Sam gurgled happily, enjoying his game. Leo shook his ears and snorted gently, edging slightly closer on Evie's knee so Sam could reach.

Evie smiled down at him, hugging him tightly. Leo knew that he was home for good.

Out Now:

Pet Rescue Adventures

The
Brave
Kitten

by HOLLY WEBB

Helena loves helping out at the animal hospital where her cousin Lucy works. One day, the girls find a young cat who's been injured by a car. Helena helps to care for the cat she names Caramel, but when it's time for him to go home, Caramel's owner can't be found.

Caramel doesn't want to be kept at the animal hospital, and he especially doesn't like the scratchy cast on his leg. But if no one comes forward to claim him, how will he ever have a place to call home?

HOLLY WEBB

Holly Webb started out as a children's book editor, and wrote her first series for the publisher she worked for. She has been writing ever since, with more than 100 books to her name. Holly lives in England with her husband and three young sons. She has three pet cats, who are always nosing around when Holly is trying to type on her laptop.

For more information about Holly Webb visit:

www.holly-webb.com
www.tigertalesbooks.com